Poul Anderson

HOMEBREW

HOMEBREW

By Poul Anderson

A BOSKONE BOOK

The NESFA Press

Cambridge, Massachusetts

1976

© 1976 by Poul Anderson

illustrations © by Rick Sternbach

Ballade of an Artificial Satellite, originally in THE MAGAZINE OF FANTASY AND SCIENCE FICTION, October 1958
© 1958 by Mercury Press

The First Love, originally in AMRA, v. 2, no. 12
© 1960 by G.H. Scithers

Upon the Occasion of Being Asked to Argue That Love and Marriage are Incompatible, originally in YE DRAGON RUNNERS' CHRONICLE, no. 1
© 1973 by Ann Cass

Science Fiction and Freedom, originally in SCIENCE FICTION REVIEW, no. 30
© 1969 by Richard E. Geis

Notes Toward a Definition of Science Fiction, originally in SCEINCE FICTION REVIEW, no. 43
© 1971 by Richard E. Geis

The Archetypical Holmes, originally in THE BAKER STREET JOURNAL, September 1968
© 1968 by The Baker Street Irregulars

A Blessedness of Saints, originally in VORPAL GLASS, no. 4
© 1962 by Karen Anderson

A Philosophical Dialogue, originally in OUTWORLDS, no. 8
© 1971 by William L. Bowers

Lost Secrets Revealed, originally in GALLIMAUFRY
© 1972 by Astrid Anderson

Uncleavish Truethinking, firstly in THE ANGLO-SAXON CHRONICLE, book 922, tale 7
Outgiverright © 1960 by Hardrada Bookwright Fellowship

Herrings, first four originally in SMORGASBORD
© 1959 by Poul Anderson, others new or from miscellaneous sources

ISBN # 0-915368-13-7   Finebound ISBN # 0-915368-78-1

This edition is limited to 500 numbered copies

This is copy number **78**

CONTENTS

FOREWARD	i
HOUSE RULE an original short story	1
BALLADE OF AN ARTIFICIAL SATELLITE a ballad	15
THE FIRST LOVE a poem	17
UPON THE OCCASION OF BEING ASKED TO ARGUE THAT LOVE AND MARRIAGE ARE INCOMPATIBLE a poem	19
LIMERICKS limericks	21
TWO SONGS songs	23
SCIENCE FICTION AND FREEDOM an essay	25
NOTES TOWARD A DEFINITION OF SCIENCE FICTION an article	31
THE ARCHETYPICAL HOLMES an article	37

A BLESSEDNESS OF SAINTS 47
an article

A PHILOSOPHICAL DIALOGUE 53
a story

LOST SECRETS REVEALED 59
a story

UNCLEAVISH TRUETHINKING 69
an article

HERRINGS 73
bon mot

HOMEBREW

FOREWORD

Carrying on an amiable custom, when the New England Science Fiction Association asked me to be its guest at Boskone XIII, it also wanted to publish a little book of my writings. In both cases, I thank the membership and have tried to oblige.

However, the volume presented a minor problem. Nearly everything of mine that now seems at all worth reading has been professionally done, and is either too long for this purpose or too readily available elsewhere. I finally decided that, for a representative piece of fiction, the best thing was to write a new story. Those who know *A Midsummer Tempest* will recognize the setting of "House Rule." Everyone will doubtless see its relationship to works by John Kendrick Bangs, Charles Erskine Scott Wood, Hendrik Willem van Loon, Lord Dunsany, Edmond Hamilton, and others, as well as the origin of all in a common daydream. The tradition seems to me to have further possibilities.

As for nonfiction items, a number have appeared here and there over the years, generally in amateur magazines. After eliminating the most dated and the most partisan, I still had a variety to choose from. Several have been re-edited just a bit for this collection. Some are outright *jeux d' esprit*; for instance, after more than twenty years of marriage, I certainly do *not* believe it is incompatible with love. Some are a touch more serious. "The Archetypical Holmes" falls in between; I hadn't realized before now that it contains the germ of "The Queen of Air and Darkness." A few pieces are verse.

May you enjoy them.

Poul Anderson

HOUSE RULE

Look for it anywhere, anytime, by day, by dusk, by night, up an ancient alley or out on an empty heath or in a forest where hunters whose eyes no spoor can escape nonetheless pass it by unseeing. Myself, I found its doorhandle under my fingers and its signboard creaking over my head when I was about to enter the saloon of a ship far at sea. You cannot really seek this house; it will seek you. But you must be alert for its fleeting presence, bright or curious or adventurous or desperate enough to enter, that first time. Thereafter, if you do not abuse its hospitality, you will be allowed to come back every once in a while.

The odds are all against you, of course. Few ever get this chance. Yet, since nobody knows what basis the landlord has for admitting his guests, and when asked he says merely that they are those who have good stories wherewith to pay him, you too may someday be favored. So keep yourself open to everything, and perhaps, just perhaps, you will have the great luck of joining us in that tavern called the Old Phoenix.

I'm not quite sure why the innkeeper and his wife the barmaid think I deserve it. There are countless others more worthy, throughout the countless dimensional sheaves, whom I have never met. When I suggest such a person, mine host shrugs, smiles, and amiably evades the question, a tactic in which he is skilled. Doubtless I've simply not happened on some of them. After all, a guest may only stay till the following dawn. Then the house won't reappear to him for a stretch which in my case has always been at least a month. Furthermore, I suspect that besides being at a nexus of universes, the hostel exists on several different space-time levels of its own.

Well, let's not speculate about the unanswerable. I want to tell of an incident I can't get out of my mind.

That evening would have been spectacular aplenty had nothing else gone on than my conversation with Leonardo da Vinci. I recognized that tall, golden-bearded man the instant he stepped into the taproom and shook raindrops off his cloak, and ventured to introduce myself. By and large, we're a friendly, informal bunch at the Old Phoenix. We come mainly to meet people. Besides, of the few who were already present, nobody but landlord, barmaid, and I knew Italian. Oh, Leonardo could have used Latin or French with the nun who sat offside and quietly listened to us. However, their accents would have made talk a struggle.

The goodwife was busy, pumping out beer for Erik the Red, Sancho Panza, and Nicholas van Rijn, interpreting and chattering away in early Norse, a peasant dialect of Spanish, and the argot of a spacefaring future, while now and then she helped herself to a tankardful. Mine host, among whose multiple names I generally choose Taverner, was off in a dim corner with beings I couldn't see very well, except that they were shadowy and full of small starlike sparkles. His round face was more solemn than usual, he often ran a hand across his bald pate, and the sounds that came from his mouth, answering those guests, were a ripple of trills and purrs.

Thus Leonardo and I were alone, until the nun entered and shyly settled down at our table. I include medieval varieties of French in my languages; being an habitué of the Old Phoenix mightily encourages such studies. But by then we two were so excited that, while we greeted her as courteously as Taverner expects, neither of us caught her name, and I barely noticed that within its coif her face was quite lovely. I did gather that she was from a convent at Argenteuil in the twelfth century. But she was content to sit and try to follow our discourse. Renaissance Florentinian was not hopelessly alien to her mother tongue.

The talk was mainly Leonardo's. Given a couple of goblets of wine to relax him, his mind soared and ranged like an eagle in a high wind. Tonight was his second time, and the first had naturally been such a stunning experience that he was still assimilating it. But the drink at our inn, like the food, is unearthly superb. (It should be; Taverner can ransack all the worlds, all the ages of a hypercosmos which, perhaps, is infinitely branched in its possibility-lines.) Leonardo soon felt at ease. In answer to a question, he told me that he was living in Milan in the year 1493 and was forty-one years old. This squared with what I recollected; so quite likely he was the same Leonardo as existed in my continuum. Certainly, from what he said, he was at the height of his fame, brilliance, powers, and longings.

"But why, Messer, why may you not say more?" he asked. His voice was deep and musical.

"Maybe I could," I replied. "None has ever given me a hard and fast catalogue of commandments. I imagine they judge each case singly. But . . . would *you* risk being forever barred from this place?"

His big body, richly clad though in hues that my era of synthetic dyes would have found subdued, twisted around in his chair. As his glance traveled over the taproom, I caught the nun admiring his profile — the least bit wistfully? She was indeed beautiful, I admitted to myself. A shapeless dark habit of rather smelly, surely heavy and scratchy wool could not altogether hide a slim young figure; her countenance was pale, delicately sculptured, huge-eyed. I wondered why, even in her milieu, she had taken vows.

The room enclosed us in cheer, long, wide, wainscotted in carven oak, ceiling massively beamed. A handsome stone fireplace held a blaze of well-scented logs, whose leap and crackle gave more warmth than you'd expect, just as the sconced candles gave more light. That light fell on straight chairs around small tables, armchairs by themselves, benches flanking the great central board, laid out ideally for fellowship. Along the walls, it touched books, pictures, and souvenirs from afar. At one end, after glowing across the bar where my lady hostess stood between the beer pumps and the racked bottles and vessels, it lost itself beyond an open doorway; but I made out a stair going up to clean, unpretentious chambers where you can sleep if you like. (People seldom do. The company is too good, the hours too precious.) Windows are always shuttered, I suppose because they would not look out over any of the worlds on which the front door opens, but onto something quite peculiar. That thought makes the inside feel still more snug.

"No," Leonardo sighed. "I daresay I too will grow careful. And yet . . . 'tis hard to understand . . . if we are mainly here for colloquy, that Messer Albergatore may enjoy the spectacle and the tales, why does he set bounds on our speech? I assure you, for instance, I do not fear your telling me the date and manner of my death, if you know them. God will call me when He chooses."

"You utter a deep truth there," I said. "For I am not necessarily from your future. For all we can tell, I may be from the future of another Leonardo da Vinci, whose destiny is, or was, not yours. Hence 'twould be a pointless unpleasantness to discuss certain matters."

"But what of the rest?" he protested. "You bespeak flying machines, automatons, elixirs injected into the flesh which prevent illness — oh, endless wonders — Why must you merely hint?"

I said into his intensity: "Messer, you have the intellect to see the reason. If I gave you over-much knowledge or foresight, what might ensue? We lack wisdom and restraint, we mortals. Taverner has a — a license? — to entertain certain among us. But it must strictly be entertainment. Nothing decisive may happen here. We meet and part as in dreams, we at the Old Phoenix."

"What then can we do?" he demanded.

"Why, there are all the arts, there are stories real and imaginary, there are the eternal riddles of our nature and purpose and meaning, there are songs and games and jests and simply being together — But it is wrong that I act pompous toward you. I feel most honored and humble, and would like naught better than to hear whatever you wish to say."

Humanly pleased, he answered, "Well, if you'll not tell me how the flying machine works — and, indeed, I can understand that if you did, 'twould avail me little, who lack the hoarded lore and instrumentalities of four or five hundred years — pray continue as you were when I interrupted. Finish relating your adventure."

I reminisced about a flight which had been forced down above the Arctic Circle, and how some Eskimos had helped us. His inquiries concerning them were keen, and led him on to experiences of his own, and to remarks about the variety and strangeness of man — As I said, had nothing else happened, this would still have been among the memorable evenings of my life.

The door opened and closed. We heard a footfall, caught a whiff of city streets which also served as garbage dumps and sewers, glimpsed crowded wooden houses on a cloudy day. The man who had appeared was rather short by my standards or against Leonardo, and middle-aged to gauge by features deeply lined though still sharply cut. Grizzled brown hair fell past his ears from under a flat velvet cap. He wore a monastic robe, with rosary and crucifix, but shoes and hose rather than sandals. His form was slender and straight, his gaze extraordinarily vivid.

Taverner excused himself from his conversation and hurried across the floor to give greeting. "Ah, welcome, welcome anew," he said in Old French — *langue d'oïl*, to be exact. "At yonder table sit two gentlemen whose companionship will surely pleasure you." He took the monk's arm. "Come, let me introduce you, my learned Master Abélard—"

The nun's voice cut through his. She surged to her feet; the chair clattered behind her. "Pier!" she cried. "O Jésu, O Maria, Pier!"

And he stood where he was for an instant as if a sword in his guts had stopped him. Then: "Héloise," cracked out of his throat. "But thou art dead." He crossed himself, over and over. "Hast thou, thou, thou come back to comfort me, Héloise?"

Taverner looked disconcerted. He must have forgotten her presence. The noise and dice-casting at the bar died away. The starry gray ones became still. Alone the hearthfire spoke.

"No, what art thou saying, I, I am alive, Pier," the nun stammered. "But thou, my poor hurt darling —" She stumbled toward him. I saw how he half flinched, before he gathered courage and held out his arms.

They met, and embraced, and stood like that: until our plump, motherly barmaid suddenly shouted, "Well, good for you, dears!" They didn't notice, they had nobody but each other.

The rest of us eased a trifle. Evidently this wasn't a bad event. Erik lifted his drinking horn, Sancho guffawed at such behavior of ecclesiastics, van Rijn held out his mug for a refill, the strangers in the corner rustled and twinkled, Taverner wryly shrugged.

Leonardo leaned across the table and whispered to me, "Did I hear aright? Are those in truth Héloise and Abélard?"

"They must be," I answered, and knew not what to feel. "Belike not from your history or mine, however."

He had grasped the idea of universes parallel in multi-dimensional reality, in some of which magic worked, in some of which it did not, in some of which King Arthur or Orlando Furioso had actually lived, in some of which he himself had not. Now he murmured, "Well, quickly, lest we say unwitting a harmful thing, let's compare what our chronicles tell about them."

"Peter Abélard was the greatest Scholastic of his century," ran from me, while I tried to take my eyes off the weeping pair and could not. "He was in his forties when he met Héloise, a girl in her twenties. She was the niece and ward of a powerful, high-born canon. They fell in love, had a child, couldn't marry because of his career in the Church but — Anyway, her uncle found out and was enraged. He hired a gang of bullies to waylay Abélard and castrate him. After that, Héloise entered a convent — against her uncle's wish, I believe — and never saw her lover again. But the bond that held them was unchanged — the world will always remember the letters that passed between them — and in my day they lie buried together."

Leonardo nodded. "Yes, that sounds like what I read. I seem to recall that they did marry, albeit secretly."

"Perhaps my memory is at fault."

"Or mine. It was long ago. For us. God in Heaven, though, they two yonder —!"

Maybe they consciously recalled this was the single place they could meet; or maybe they, like most people in their age, had scant notion of privacy; or maybe they didn't give a damn. I heard what they blurted forth through their tears.

They were from separate time-lines. She might belong to Leonardo's and mine, if ours were the same; her story was familiar to us both. But he, he was still a whole man. For him, three years before, she had died in childbirth.

Meanwhile Taverner led them to an offside couch; and the barmaid fetched refreshments, which they didn't see; and host and hostess breathed to them what no one else could hear. Not that anybody wanted to. As if half ashamed, they at the bar returned to their boozing, Leonardo and I to our talk; they in the corner waited silent.

My companion soon lost his embarrassment. Tender-heartedness is not notably a Renaissance trait. Since we knew equally little about the branchings of existence, we were free to wonder aloud about them. He got onto constructing such a world-of-if (suppose Antony had triumphed at Actium, because the library at Alexandria had not caught fire when Julius Caesar laid siege, and in it were Heron's plans for a submersible warcraft . . . well, conceivably, somewhere among the dimensions it *did* happen) that I too, chiming in here and there, well-nigh lost awareness of the nun and her Schoolman.

Again the door interrupted us — half an hour later, an hour, I'm not sure. This time I spied a lawn, trees, ivy-covered red brick buildings, before it shut. The man who had arrived was old and not tall, yet much robustness remained to him. He wore an open-necked shirt, fuzzy sweater, faded slacks, battered sneakers. A glory of white hair framed the kind of plain, gentle, but thoughtful and characterful Jewish face that Rembrandt liked to portray.

He saw Héloise and Abélard together, and smiled uncertainly. *"Guten Abend,"* he ventured; and in English: "Good evening. Maybe I had better not —"

"Ah, do stay!" exclaimed Taverner, hurrying toward him, while the eyes popped in van Rijn's piratical visage and my pulse ran wild.

Taverner took the newcomer by the elbow and steered him toward us. "By all means, do," he urged. "True, we've had a scene, but harmless, yes, I'd say benign. And here's a gentleman I know you've been wanting to meet." He reached our table and made a grand flourish. "Messer Leonardo da Vinci . . . Herr Doktor Albert Einstein. . . ." I suppose he included me.

Of course, the Italian had not heard of the Jew, but he sensed what was afoot and bowed deeply. Einstein, more diffident, nevertheless responded with similar grace and sat down amidst polite noises all around. "Do you mind if I smoke?" he asked. We didn't, so he kindled a pipe while the barmaid brought new drinks. Neither of my tablemates did more than sip, however, and I wasn't about to spoil this for myself by getting drunk the way they were doing over at the bar.

Besides, I must be interpreter. Einstein's Italian was limited, and of a date centuries later than Leonardo's, who had neither German nor English. *I* interpreted. Do you see why I will never risk my standing at the Old Phoenix?

They needed a while to warm up. Einstein was eager to learn what this or that cryptic notation of Leonardo's referred to. But Leonardo must have Einstein's biography related to him.

When he realized what that signified, his blue eyes became blowtorches, and I had trouble following every word that torrented from him. We thus got some pauses. Furthermore, occasionally even those chain lightning minds must halt and search before going on. Hence, unavoidably, I noticed Héloise and Abélard anew.

They sat kissing, whispering, trembling. This was the sole night they could have, she alive, he his entire self — the odds against their ever chancing to meet here were unmeasurably huge — and what was allowed them, by the law of their hostel and the law of their holy orders? Tick, said a grandfather clock by the wall, tick, tick; here too, a night is twelve hours long.

Taverner scuttled around in the unobtrusive way he can don when he wants to. They started trading songs at the bar. The taproom is big enough that that doesn't annoy anyone who hasn't a very good ear; and Einstein and Leonardo, who did, were too engaged with each other.

What does the smile mean upon Mona Lisa and your several Madonnas?

Will you give to me again that melody of Bach's?

How did you fare under Sforza, how under Borgia, how under King Francis?

How did you fare in Switzerland, how against Hitler, how with Roosevelt?

What physical considerations led you to think men might build wings?

What evidence proves that the earth goes a-round the sun, that light has a finite speed, that the stars are also suns?

What makes you doubt the finiteness of the universe?

Well, sir, why have you not analyzed your concept of space-time as follows?

Taverner and the barmaid spoke low behind their hands. Finally she went to Héloise and Abélard. "Go on upstairs," she said through tears of her own. "You've only this while, and it's wearing away."

He looked up like a blind man. "We took vows," came from his lips.

Héloise closed them with hers. "Thou didst break thine before," she told him, "and we praised the goodness of God."

"Go, go," said the barmaid. Almost by herself, she raised them to their feet. I saw them leave, I heard them on the stairs.

And then Leonardo: "Doctor Alberto, you waste your efforts." He grimaced; the hands knotted around his goblet. "I cannot follow your mathematics, your logic. I have not the knowledge —"

But Einstein leaned forward, and his voice too was less than steady. "You have the brain. And, yes, a fresh view, an insight not blinkered by four centuries of progress point by point . . . down a single road, when we know in this room there are many, many. . . ."

"You cannot explain to me in a few hours —"

"No, but you can get a general idea of what I mean, and I think you, out of everybody who ever lived, can see where . . . where I am astray — and from me, you can carry back home —"

Leonardo flamed.

"No."

That was Taverner. He had come up on the empty side of our table; and he no longer seemed stumpy or jolly.

"No, gentlemen," he said in language after language. His tone was not stern, it was regretful.

But it never wavered. "I fear I must ask you to change the subject. You would learn more than should be. Both of you."

We stared at him, and the silence around us turned off the singing. Leonardo's countenance froze. Finally Einstein smiled lopsidedly, scraped back his chair, stood, knocked the dottle from his pipe. Its odor was bittersweet. "My apologies, Herr Gastwirt," he said in his soft fashion. "You are right. I forgot." He bowed. "This evening has been an honor and a delight. Thank you."

Turning, his small stooped form departed.

When the door had shut on him, Leonardo sat unmoving for another while. Taverner threw me a rueful grin and went back to his visiting mysteries. The men at the bar, who had sensed a problem and quieted down, now cheered up and grew rowdier yet. When Mrs. Hauksbee walked in, they cheered.

Leonardo cast his goblet on the floor. Glass flew outward, wine fountained red. "Héloise and Abélard!" he roared. "*They* will have had their night!"

BALLADE
OF AN ARTIFICIAL SATELLITE

Thence they sailed far to the southward along the land, and came to a ness; the land lay upon the right; there were long and sandy strands. They rowed to land, and found there upon the ness the keel of a ship, and called the place Keelness, and the strands they called Wonderstrands for it took long to sail by them.
— Thorfinn Karlsefni's voyage to Vinland, as related in the saga of Erik the Red

One inland summer I walked through rye,
a wind at my heels that smelled of rain
and harried white clouds through a whistling sky
where the great sun stalked and shook his mane
and roared so brightly across the grain
it burned and shimmered like alien sands. —
Ten years old, I saw down a lane
the thunderous light on Wonderstrands.

In ages before the world ran dry,
what might the mapless not contain?
Atlantis gleamed like a dream to die,
Avalon lay under faerie reign,
Cíbola guarded a golden plain,
Tir-nan-Og was fair-locked Fand's,
sober men saw from a gull's-road wain
the thunderous light on Wonderstrands.

Such clanging countries in cloudland lie;
but men grew weary and they grew sane
and they grew grown — and so did I —
and knew Tartessus was only Spain.
No galleons call at Taprobane
(Ceylon, with English); no queenly hands
wear gold from Punt; nor sees the Dane
the thunderous light on Wonderstrands.

Ahoy, Prince Andros Horizon's-bane!
They always wait, the elven lands.
An evening planet gives again
the thunderous light on Wonderstrands.

THE FIRST LOVE

(This is my translation of a poem from the Old Norse. Olaf the Stout, later to be St. Olaf [995-1030], King of Norway, had once been betrothed to Ingigerdh, a Swedish princess; but enmity with her father caused the match to fall through, and she married Grand Prince Yaroslav of Kievan Russia. Years afterward, while he was an exile taking refuge with her husband, Olaf stood on a hill outside Novgorod one day when Ingigerdh went riding by. "Her form was bowed and her face was faded," says the saga. He looked on her and made these lines.)

> From my hill I followed
> the faring, when on horseback
> lightly did the lovely
> let herself be outborne.
> And her shining eyes
> did all my joy bereave me:
> known it is, to no one
> naught of sorrow happens.

Formerly in fairness,
filled with golden blossoms,
trees stood green and trembling,
tall above the jarldom.
Soon their leaves grew sallow,
silently, in Russia.
Only gold now garlands
Ingigerdha's forehead.

UPON THE OCCASION OF BEING ASKED TO ARGUE THAT LOVE AND MARRIAGE ARE INCOMPATIBLE

Love is no lady, but a wench with wings,
fickle and fleet, the child of wind and sky,
cool as a fall where tumbling water rings,
brazen as sunlight and like moonglow shy.
Love is a hawk no man may hope to tame.
She is not chased, but hers is the attack.
Love is no bride who meekly yields her name,
nor, being winged, lies always on her back.
How shall you cage the river or the gale?
How shall you pluck and lifelong keep alive
blossoms in bowls where air is walled and stale?
Love comes to whom she will, not those who strive.
Therefore, my sweet, be in no haste to marry,
so it may be that Love will deign to tarry.

LIMERICKS

An astronomer's swift limousine
went through a red light in Racine.
    He was going so fast
    that the light which he passed,
through Doppler effect, showed as green.

A foolish young chemist named Kroll
heated fulminate up in a bowl.
    Without distillation
    he got separation,
i.e. of his body and soul.

(Dedicated to Fritz Leiber)
A mathematician named Jones
was fonder of cubes than of cones.
    Said he on his rambles:
    "When I travels, I gambles.
Gonna roll them Napierian bones!"

The jury was out all the day.
Next lunchtime, the foreman did say:
    "Bring us five ham-on-ryes,
    four chicken pot pies,
two pastramis, and one bale of hay."

(Dedicated to Robert A. Heinlein)
Poor Joe-Jim, with one extra head,
could not have a woman in bed.
    "Since I cannot abet you,
    I never will let you,
for I'm no voyeur," each head said.

There was a young man of Calais
who considered himself a gourmet,
    eating crocodile roast
    and flies' eggs upon toast.
His sex life was more recherché.

(Dedicated to Isaac Asimov)
On Lagash, after Stars come in view,
the rebuilders by daylight are few.
    Staying cultured is hard
    when all cities are charred
and paternities dubious, too.

TWO SONGS
(Melodies: obvious)

1

I wandered today to the hill, Maggie,
although it has been bulldozed low.
The creek's thick with gunk from the mill, Maggie,
the tract houses jammed row on row.
The air is mephitic and gray, Maggie,
the grass dead where concrete has been flung.
Let us sing of the progress they've made, Maggie,
since you and I were young.

2

Black bodies give off radiation,
and ought to continuously.
Black bodies give off radiation,
but do it by Planck's theory.

   (Chorus) Bring back, bring back,
                 oh, bring back that old continuity!
                 Bring back, bring back,
                 oh, bring back Clerk Maxwell to me!

Though now we have Schrödinger functions,
dividing up h by 2π,
that damn differential equation
still has no solution for ψ.

(Chorus)

SCIENCE FICTION AND FREEDOM

A number of years ago, in a letter to PITFCS (that's *Proceedings of the Institute for Twenty-first Century Studies*, it was kind of a fanzine for pros, and the acronym was pronounced exactly as you think) my friend Winston P. Sanders wondered why this or that writer was so often called "courageous." As long as we have the First Amendment, he said, what does anybody risk by writing anything that isn't libelous, except a rejection slip? Even pornographers, who in those days might seem brave since they did chance prosecution, seldom got into trouble; only their publishers did, as another man pointed out to Sanders with fiendish glee.

Since then it has occurred to me that a person who writes part time — which is the usual case — might conceivably find his regular job at stake, if he gets something into print that his boss doesn't like. Still, the guts involved here are of a different type from what the critics seem to mean, if literary critics ever mean anything. They are the guts of any free man who speaks his piece. The fact that this particular fellow speaks it on the typewriter rather than with his mouth looks almost incidental.

So does writing have any unique occupational hazard?

Poverty, eyestrain, ulcers, insomnia, nightmares, melancholia, alcoholism, loneliness, paranoia . . . no, nothing off a list like that is peculiar to writers, and not all writers suffer from such-like ills. Probably the majority don't. In the main, we seem to be a disgustingly cheerful lot.

About the only risk I can think of, then, which we run to a greater degree than average, is enmity. (And even here we are less exposed than politicians.) Somebody will dislike what you, the writer, said — more frequently, what he thinks you said — and promptly decide that you are a revolving son of a bitch.

Or, if he is of temperate character, he will assume that you have some bastardly opinions, however pleasant you may be in person. Sometimes, of course, he's right. But often he is only reacting because you happened to jab him in one of his tenderest prejudices.

What brought this on was taking the late Norbert Wiener's *The Human Use of Human Beings* off the shelf and coming upon mention of Kipling's early science fiction story "With the Night Mail." Now before anyone accuses me of accusing Norbert Wiener of anything, I hasten to say that he was an admirable man and all I want to do is express polite disagreement about something as a takeoff point for something else. "It is rather a Fascist picture which Kipling gives us," he wrote, "and this is understandable in view of his intellectual presuppositions." (In justice to both, I should also quote the last sentence in the paragraph, following several technical arguments: "Nevertheless, with these natural reservations, Kipling had the poet's insight, and the things he has foreseen are rapidly coming to pass.")

Kipling? Fascist? Huh?

Well, for a while during the *Starship Troopers* hooraw, some people were saying that about Heinlein, too. Some still are. Actually, Kipling and Heinlein have been among the most eloquent advocates that the cause of freedom has had in this century. The society of *Starship Troopers* turns out on examination to be more free than our own today. (Whether it would long remain thus is an entirely separate question.) So does the society of "With the Night Mail," though this is made plainest in the sequel "As Easy As ABC," which Dr. Wiener had perhaps not read — a story which points out, as de Jouvenel was to do decades later at book length in his brilliant study *On Power*, that democracy has at least as much potential for becoming tyranny as any other form of government.

As far as that goes, I lay claim to the same libertarian advocacy if not to the eloquence, and have also been called a fascist. What do we three, and other writers like us, have in common that provokes this kind of thing?

After pondering it for a beer or two, I came up with a tentative answer. There are certain qualities which a leftist friend of mine calls the fascist virtues. In fact, they are not *per se*. Their explicit formulation goes back to Sparta and to Plato's *Republic*, and they were part though not all of the morality of the authors of the United States Constitution. But in our era they have been more loudly exalted by totalitarians than by others. That's a pity; but let's not make them guilty by association. They are quite real virtues — discipline, courage, devotion to the community and its ideals above self, and (here is where they part company with the Communist virtues) a readiness to live with tragedy, public more than private, a readiness to admit that often the community itself must try in stumbling mortal fashion to identify what is the lesser wrong and then perpetrate it.

Now obviously these are insufficient by themselves for a civilized human being. We need compassion and inquiring minds as well, to name only two things. But to get to the point, those of us who are interested enough in preserving liberty to make a study of the relevant phenomena have, in some cases, reached the conclusion that the Spartan virtues are necessary for the long-time survival of this institution. Not sufficient, I repeat; not sufficient by several light-years; but necessary. Feeling that they are dangerously underemphasized in modern Western society, we sometimes lay stress on them in our writings. This, I suspect, is what makes our more excitable readers pounce to the conclusion that we are preaching fascism.

No such thing! In a dictatorship, virtue is imposed from above and consists essentially of conformity. The free man has to produce virtue from within himself. But how can he, if he's never learned it in the first place? This is why my theories on the upbringing of children run a little toward strictness (and a lot toward love). To be free as adults, they have to have self-discipline, and that has to be acquired early in life. Furthermore, freedom without a corresponding sense of responsibility is bound to lead to abuses whose correction demands measures curtailing freedom.

Yet in the not so long run, throughout some five thousand years of recorded history, corrections of that kind have always turned into worse abuses. Never trust a government. The fact that it may (perhaps) be a necessary evil does not change the fact that it is an evil. Let's bend our efforts toward outgrowing the necessity — starting not in some grandiosely reformed distant future, but right now.

End of sermon. Fill my glass, will you, while you're on your feet?

NOTES TOWARD A DEFINITION
OF SCIENCE FICTION

There seem to be as many definitions of science fiction as there are definers, and — in spite of some undeservedly kind remarks by A.J. Budrys — I am not about to add to their number. A field which can include *Brave New World* and *A Canticle for Leibowitz* and Venus Equilateral and Captain Future obviously has no single definition. A bitter old Jewish saying goes: "A Jew is anybody whom somebody else says is a Jew." Sf is in a comparable boat, inasmuch as the literati still frequently declare that nothing which is good can, by definition, be sf. But this attitude is breaking down. In fact, we are in such danger of becoming respectable that I tend to agree with what got scrawled on the blackboard after a session at a Secondary Universe conference, where academic types had earnestly sought for critical standards appropriate to us: GET SCIENCE FICTION OUT OF THE CLASSROOM AND BACK IN THE GUTTER WHERE IT BELONGS.

So, anything is sf which I say is sf. By and large, my list is the same as that of any other long-term buff. But what do the stories to which we point have in common?

Though not a rider on the creamed chicken circuit, I do give occasional lectures, seminars, and the like. (Among other reasons, it always heartens me to get out among students and rediscover that the large majority are perfectly decent, reasonable, clean, and likeable human beings. The future they will shape if they get the chance will be different from the past — hasn't the future always been? — and no doubt I will disapprove of some elements; but on balance, I don't expect to be more appalled than I am at present, and quite possibly less.)

When introducing the topic of sf to such an audience, if sf is the topic, I call it "a set of literary techniques." It is not basically different from other categories of fiction, which are not basically different from each other. In fact, categorization is a strictly twentieth-century idiocy. Still, when the story to be told or the point to be made or the atmosphere to be created demands certain techniques for maximum effectiveness, we have sf.

These are by no means the only techniques suitable to that kind of story. Rather, the current revitalization of our field is due largely to the introduction of methods and approaches which have long been known elsewhere. Peter Beagle once remarked that he'd read sf as a boy, then dropped it for many years, then lately come back to it, and by gosh, he said, meanwhile those guys had discovered the stream of consciousness!

Obviously, however, no story can employ the whole range of available devices. Some will always be inappropriate. For instance, the minute cataloguing of everyday detail is fine in a typical *New Yorker* story, if you like *New Yorker* stories, but would hopelessly bog down a fast-action detective yarn — though the point-by-point description of certain matters is integral to the police procedural novel. The degree of it in a sf piece depends on what the writer has set out to do. Thus, Heinlein often uses it, Sturgeon rarely; yet the latter can vividly evoke a scene by mentioning just two or three well-chosen things. The difference is in the kind of effect these men are respectively after.

The techniques peculiarly appropriate to sf seem to me to fall in two broad classes, the employment of certain symbols and the expression of a certain attitude.

The symbols are an expansible group. The healthy eras of sf have been characterized by the introduction and exploration of new ones, the dull eras by the mechanical reiteration of old ones. Familiar symbols include spaceships, distant planets, nonhuman intelligences, vast forces, the future and its civilizations or savageries, time travel. They differ from their counterparts in "straight" literature because they don't employ anything presently in existence, and often they employ things unlikely ever to be in existence.

An Apollo command module or an IBM computer or a nuclear detonation is real. It might occur in a sf story which takes off from the here-and-now, just as an automobile might, but it is functionally different in the story from, say, an interstellar liner or a robot with awareness or a supernova which destroys whole worlds. The spaceship, for example, is a symbol of travel, adventure, achievement; or the writer can make it stand for evil, like one of Bradbury's vessels full of looters and litterers; the point is that it can call forth emotions in predictable ways, like a familiar few bars of music woven into another, larger composition. Now of course a good writer could use an Apollo to that end, or a dogsled crossing Arctic ice. But if he wants to bring in more than this — the emotion of marvel or terror, say, to be generated by the symbolic structure of an unearthly planet — then as a rule logic requires him to use sf's standard ultra-developed spaceship for his Voyage symbol.

As for the attitude expressed, I'd say that sf characteristically assumes that, however strange it may be, creation makes sense; it is governed by laws, and these laws are discoverable by man. This does not mean bland optimism. In fact, some of sf's greatest successes have been tragedies, wherein ruin results either from man's failure to grasp and/or use the realities — e.g., "The Cold Equations," not to mention tales of atomic wars and anti-Utopias and whatever — or else from doom being in the nature of things — e.g., "Twilight." The essential is only that we echo Einstein: "Raffiniert ist der Herr Gott, aber boshaft ist Er nicht."

Our story postulates can be quite outré. Actually, the real-world plausibility of ghosts is slightly better than that of such sf standbys as faster-than-light or time travel.* Yet ghosts almost all belong to fantasy. Why? I think sf takes the attitude, tacit where not explicit, that we may come upon many remarkable phenomena, which will quite revolutionize our thinking, but they'll nevertheless include what we know today; there will have been the same kind of intellectual continuity that there was between Newtonian and modern physics. The fantasy writer doesn't care. He postulates as he pleases. Though he may be rigorously logical in tracing out the consequences of these postulates, he is under no necessity of assuming that they can ever be fitted into the body of scientific knowledge. When he does make this assumption, he is automatically writing sf. For instance, I've seen ghost stories which "explained" the spirit in terms of forcefields or something else physical, and have even written one or two myself. In contrast, while Bradbury's fine Mars stories used the symbolism of sf, he refused (probably rightly in his case) to throw in any line of gobbledygook that would "explain" away the findings of astronomy; thus in attitude he was being a fantasy writer.

Needless to say, the sf attitude is not unique to it. But sf does seem to employ the outlook more commonly and more emphatically than is the case elsewhere. Likewise, while the spaceship as symbol may be functionally identical with a caravel in a historical romance, each has at least the potential of conveying something additional by association (such as the thrill of intellection versus the thrill of using sheer physical strength) which the other can't carry as well. Nowadays some motifs, such as Travel and Strangeness, are more frequent in sf than elsewhere.

Nevertheless, it shades into the rest of literature. What peculiarities it has are of degree, not of kind.

---

*Since this essay was first published, both these motifs are beginning to look scientifically a bit less disreputable. However, this is a very recent development, and no doubt the bulk of the evidence is still against it.

THE ARCHETYPICAL HOLMES

The work of Carl Gustav Jung does not seem to belong in our era. Some would make it a relic, albeit a fascinating and suggestive one, of an earlier and more credulous stage in human development. Others maintain that our culture has not yet advanced to the point where we can fully comprehend and use the insights of the late great Swiss psychiatrist.

For whatever it may be worth, which isn't likely much, I take a middle position. On the one hand, it is difficult for a hard-boiled, physical-science-oriented, show-me positivist to swallow such Jungian notions as the racial unconscious. They don't seem to refer to anything observable. I prefer incontrovertible, understandable realities, such as particles that have no mass, stars that are too big to shine, and, of course, Sherlock Holmes.

On the other hand, no one can deny that Jung performed a mighty service. He broke free of the rigid Freudian mold, he made a fresh and still valuable classification of personality types, he founded a school of psychoanalysis that has helped many people, and on and on. The Jungian concept that should be of special interest to Sherlockians is the archetype.

Webster defines "archetype" as "the original pattern of which all things of the same species are representations or copies; original idea, model, or type." Jung gave it a less strictly Platonic meaning. In his researches he found that certain images recur again and again in the mind, in many different forms but always identifiably the same. He found them not merely in his European patients, but in healthy people of every race and background, in dreams, reveries, fantasies, myths, religions, and mystical experiences. Among these figures he identified the earth mother, the persona, the anima, and the shadow. We have only to think about them to see how fundamental and universal they are.

For instance, the earth mother occurs as a thousand different goddesses, from Kwan-Yin in the East to Juno in the West and on to similar deities in the Americas, Africa, and Oceania. She is also a type of woman, the big, strong, patient but indomitable heroine of innumerable novels. Now and then you meet her in some real person. Probably your own mother was the first one who gave you this impression. If you are at all introspective, you will quickly realize how the earth mother likewise pervades your dreams and your daydreams.

I think we can accept Jung's archetypes without needing his collective unconscious to explain them. They arise out of human experience, the long pilgrimage of mankind as a whole, the subtle interaction of societies and individuals, and the ordinary lives of each one of us — these lives being, after all, very much alike.

In other words, an archetype doesn't spring out full-blown, it evolves. Many influences converge to form it. At last it takes a definite shape. Then the archetype has gained power. It goes on through the centuries, in countless variant forms, all of which are traceable back to the first completely developed one. Some of these new forms are mythical, literary, or what have you. Others are real. That is to say, whenever a real person comes along who more or less fits an archetype, we will inevitably think about him in terms of that archetype, and he will even tend to act accordingly.

No doubt this sounds pretty abstract. Let me therefore give you a concrete example. To wit: Sherlock Holmes is an archetype.

That is, the general idea of a Holmesian figure had been slowly evolving for a long while. Its time was ripe in the late nineteenth century, and the elements crystallized in Sherlock Holmes, who gave them their essential eternal shape. It does not matter that he actually existed; he could just as well have been a character in a story. The point is that he expressed certain vital factors. As a result, the Holmes figure has reappeared in any number of versions already, and bids fair to go on indefinitely.

It is not easy to define the elements of Holmes. In fact, his complexity, the veil that is never lifted between the world and his ultimate self, is part of the image. But we can point to a few obvious traits.

The brilliant deductive mind; the intense concentration on any problem; the occasional furious activity; the physical courage and competence; the philosophical musings; the idealism and affection nearly always masked by sardonic reserve; the austere habits of life, relieved by a few minor vices and self-indulgences — but I need not remind you further.

Now the interesting thing for present purposes is that Holmes-like characters are hard to come by in other civilizations and earlier times. We do have ancient detective stories, like those concerning the prophet Daniel. It is said that the caliph Haroun al-Rashid often wandered around Bagdad in disguise to learn what people really were doing. Robert van Gulik's tales of Judge Dee, who made shrewd deductions, were adapted from the Chinese. But while all these, and others, contain certain aspects of Sherlock Holmes, they do not approach the totality. Nor do we find anything that suggests him among, say, the Olympian gods. Zeus is wise and powerful, Hermes is clever, Hephaestus is inventive, and so on. But the pieces are scattered, and some are missing altogether.

The most Holmesian figure I can think of, real or imaginary, in the ancient world is Archimedes. He lived in the third century B.C. and is best known popularly for his detective work when he proved that alloy had been substituted for gold in a royal crown. The legend that, when the solution hit him, he leaped from his bath and ran down the streets crying, "Eureka! I have found it!" is quite Holmesian. Not that Sherlock would ever do any such thing, but at least he was careless in his dress.

Archimedes was a brilliant mathematician (a hint of Moriarty there?) but also a research scientist, an artificer, a helper of his country in its hour of peril. He is said to have been ascetic and brusque. He was killed when he wouldn't leave the diagram he was studying to go away with conquering enemy soldiers.

Archimedes might thus have become the seminal figure we are after. But he was too isolated. The decaying Hellenistic world, its intellectually unenterprising Roman successor, had small use for his kind of man. So, if anything, he is especially clear in our minds today because he fits an archetype that has evolved after his death.

It does seem to be one which originated in Western civilization. Our Celtic and Nordic predecessors already show the germ of it. Is Merlin, the magician confidant of King Arthur, not Holmesian in several ways? We think of him as gaunt, enigmatic, possessed of knowledge and intelligence such as were granted no one else. Incidentally, for him too there was just one woman, of dubious associations and dangerous ambitions.

Still more Holmesian is the Northern god Odin, or Wotan if you prefer the operatic name. He is described as both wise and shrewd, benevolent and terrible; he fights the powers of evil with cunning rather than with spear, yet he can wield that well if he desires; he is tall and lean and dignified, though a few comic stories are told about him; he presides over the riotous feasting in Valhalla but does not otherwise join in; he is an inventor of magical techniques, and a linguist who first read the runes; he is the brooding foreknower of the future.

As European history proceeds, we find men appearing oftener and oftener, in fact and fiction, who look increasingly Holmesian. To name a few, consider Roger Bacon in the Middle Ages and Francis Bacon in the Elizabethan era. Down south we get personages such as Machiavelli, a much-maligned thinker who was simply a frank realist, and Leonardo da Vinci, who I once suggested might be a collateral ancestor of Sherlock Holmes. The type becomes rare again during the upheavals of the Reformation, but in the Enlightenment it flourishes more luxuriantly than ever before. Newton and Leibniz are obviously proto-Holmeses, as well as Locke, Hume, and above all Voltaire; America produced such as Hamilton, Jay, and Marshall.

The Napoleonic era in Europe did not have many. Those who were around at the time were mostly leftovers from the Enlightenment. Apparently Holmes personalities belong to relatively settled and civilized milieus. Hence they are scarce in the earlier nineteenth century, which was dominated by Romanticism. But presently a long, stable peace brought forth this sort of man afresh, and plentifully. Again making a brief random selection, consider Disraeli, T.H. Huxley, Clerk Maxwell, John Stuart Mill, Jeremy Bentham, and, inevitably, Dr. Joseph Bell.

Meanwhile, on the literary side, Holmes had been foreshadowed by such as Reynard the Fox in folk tales, Shakespeare's Hamlet, Voltaire's own Zadig, Mark Twain's Pudd'nhead Wilson and Connecticut Yankee, Poe's Dupin, Stevenson's Prince Florizel, and others. And now we are well into the age of Victoria.

The hour had arrived. The Master came into being. We will pause for a moment in honor.

* * * * * * * * * * * * * * * * * *

It would take far more scholarship and patience than are mine to explore the immediate effects of the coalescence of the archetype. Clearly, almost every detective of the classic period is essentially Holmes. Some are good expressions of the basic form, like Hercule Poirot; some are not so good, like Philo Vance. But I need not elaborate for this readership.

It would be interesting to trace the archetype elsewhere. Curiously enough, I don't think you find it in H.G. Wells. He claimed to be a rationalist, but in fact he was too passionate, too much a believer, too little guarded by Holmes' streak of healthy cynicism. By contrast, in his life even more than in his writings, George Bernard Shaw strikes me as very Holmesian. Kipling employed the archetype several times, notably when he created Strickland and Lurgan Sahib in his stories of India. The Head of the school in *Stalky and Co.* is rather a Sherlockian figure, and so on occasion is the chaplain, whom you will remember as getting the boys to do things that needed doing but were impossible for an adult. To some extent *Stalky* is a Holmesian narrative told from the viewpoint of the Baker Street Irregulars.

Unfortunately, the Victorian-Edwardian environment did not last, but went out in the catastrophe of the First World War. The Master made one of his rare mistakes when he predicted that that conflict would be cleansing. Instead, this was when Western civilization cut its own throat. It has been bleeding to death ever since. We have already remarked that the Holmes archetype feels most at home in a free but essentially orderly society — just as the earth mother manifests herself most frequently in cultures that do not lock women away in some version of purdah.

An enclave of the orderliness prevalent before 1914 remains, to a degree, in the sciences. Hence it is not surprising that many scientists and engineers have much in common with the Master. Their work depends on both intellect and physique; they tend to be devoted, clean-living, but comparatively aloof and eccentric men. To name just one, I might observe that the oceanographer and deep-sea explorer Jacques-Yves Cousteau goes so far as to look like Sherlock Holmes!

On the whole, though, few Victorian-type adventurers are left. This is yet more obvious in literature than in life. The protagonist — I won't say hero — of the average "serious" novel is a sniveling little neurotic that Lestrade himself wouldn't wipe his feet on. The protagonist of the mystery and suspense story is apt to be a drab organization man, a psychopathic brute, or a grubby and fearful espionage agent. I don't say this is good or bad. No doubt it reflects the reality of our times. But there are those among us who wish the reality were a bit different.

Therefore we turn to sheer fantasy for escape, including that branch of fantasy known as science fiction. And here we find the Holmes archetype enjoying very good health, thank you. Indeed, it dominates the field so thoroughly that other types of hero are in danger of becoming extinct.

Take, for instance, J.R.R. Tolkien's *The Lord of the Rings*. Are not Strider and, especially, Gandalf Holmes personalities? For that matter, is Sauron not another Moriarty, and are the hobbits not a multiple John H. Watson? The popularity of this epic, particularly among younger readers, is encouraging. It suggests that man has not altogether abandoned the wish for a sane and decent order of things.

Science fiction in the strict sense is positively loaded with Holmes types. Among so many, I might arbitrarily mention Sir Austin Cardynge, the "lean gray tomcat" of E.E. Smith's Lensman series; or Jay Score, the gentle robot created by Eric Frank Russell; or Susan Calvin, a female version by Isaac Asimov. But mainly, I wish to point out that one science fiction personality, who has seized the mass imagination as no other has ever done, is pure Holmes. I refer to Mr. Spock on the television show "Star Trek."

Tune it in sometime, if you haven't already — above all, if you can catch reruns of the first two seasons, when the action was live and the plots were still fairly good. Mr. Spock is only second in command of the spaceship *Enterprise*, but it is plain that Captain Kirk depends on him every bit as much as a certain gracious lady did on the Master. Spock exalts the intellect and derides the emotions in the strictest tradition; but, also in that tradition, he obviously has intense feelings that never ordinarily reveals. He is courteous but distant where women are concerned, except on one or two occasions when he can no longer help himself. He has the catlike neatness and curiosity of a Holmes (and, incidentally, the supercats in Clarence Day's little essay *This Simian World* are rather Holmesian).

Spock exasperates his less intellectual companions, but usually meets their sarcasms with a ready and biting wit. At the same time, he is athletic, cool and capable in danger. He is withdrawn, austere, philosophical, and, as played by Leonard Nimoy, allowing for the uniform and the pointed ears, presents an excellent physical image of Sherlock Holmes.

One thing he does lack on the show, and that is a Watson. But in real life he has thousands, as devout as any Baker Street Irregular. Some of them publish magazines about him. Though they include both sexes and every age, he has a special attraction for young girls.

Whenever Mr. Nimoy is next looking for a role, I wish he would consider the fact that he is potentially the perfect successor to Basil Rathbone, and that you would write to the networks and movie companies saying so. I further suggest that his popularity is another hopeful sign. The girls who today adore this nearly 200 proof Holmesian archetype will be the mothers of tomorrow. They, their husbands, and their children may yet create a new age of Victoria.

A BLESSEDNESS OF SAINTS

Some years ago, the University of California library had an exhibit of old maps. Colorful things. Modern charts don't compare. Coordinate grids make a drab substitute for wind gods going oompa, oompa, and contour lines are no fair exchange at all for the actual contours on some of those mermaids. To hell with radicals like Goldwater — let's bring back the *eighteenth* century! But I digress. What I started out to mention was a Spanish map of the western hemisphere, dated 17something and not very detailed. One place they did show was Cape Canaveral. And out in the Pacific they had, neatly labeled, the Islas de San Dwich.

When Anthony Boucher heard about this, he laughed and said that must be a Catalan saint. It's tempting to develop the hagiography further . . . Dwich, apostle to the Anthropophagi, martyred by being sliced very thin and served on rye bread with mustard . . . he did persuade the cannibals to postpone his execution twenty-four hours, till Saturday . . . But this moving tale had better not be written.

There are far too many spurious saints already.

Some of them are etymological too, like that St. Sophia to whom the cathedral in Constantinople was not dedicated. (For the benefit of any barbarians in my audience, though surely there are none, "Hagia Sophia" means "Holy Wisdom.") I've also heard of St. Trinity (Hagia Triada), St. Saviour, and a St. Cross believed to have been a Frenchman. James Branch Cabell mentions a St. Undecimilla whose name gave rise to the legend of the eleven thousand virgins — for whom, by the way, the Virgin Islands were named — and say, couldn't a martini be called a vergin? — But I'm digressing again.

A vast number of saints got into the calendar during the Dark and Middle Ages, before canonization had become a controlled procedure. Some were historical enough, though their claims to sainthood are, to put it politely, arguable. St. Olaf of Norway is still accepted, but even in medieval times people admitted that he didn't attain any state of grace till rather late in life. One of my ambitions is to go onto the campus of St. Olaf College, a strait-laced Lutheran institution in my home town, barricade myself on the water tower, and through a bullhorn read aloud some of the racier passages from the original chronicles of the patron — murders, robberies, booze hoistings, illegitimate son, and all.

Charlemagne was canonized by an anti-Pope at the request of Frederick Barbarossa; his festival was celebrated in some parts till fairly recently. The Byzantine Empress Zoe, whose career would have made Theodora blush, is a saint in the Eastern church though naturally not among the Romans;

likewise Alexander Nevsky, because he stopped a bunch of Catholic invaders. In late years the Vatican has been re-examining the credentials of its saints and has dropped a lot of them, especially the fictitious ones. St. Hippolytus, for instance, who was said to have been dragged to death by horses, is merely Theseus' son from pagan Greek legend. St. Philomena has likewise been declared to be fabulous. I mean fabulous in the original sense of the word. The modern sense could be applied to the legendary St. Mary the Egyptian, a pilgrim to the Holy Land who worked out her passage in an interesting capacity.

However, no right-thinking Anglophile can go along with this business of demoting St. George to apocryphal status. Impossible. Utter nonsense. St. George doubtful? Gad, sir, that sort of thing just isn't said. Least of all where the servants might overhear. Shows you how schism is bound to turn into sheer heresy, by Jove. Ever since those Romans left the C. of E. . . . . St. George for merrie England! God send the right! Death to the French! But first a pint at the George and Dragon. . . .

One perfectly genuine saint often confuses people. The Scandinavians have an ancient custom of lighting bonfires on Midsummer Eve; but who's this here Sankt Hans they talk about?

Getting back to fictional ones, though, it's surprising how many purely literary instances I can think of offhand. Norman Douglas' *South Wind* has a St. Dodecanus who — even in the probability-world of the novel — looks implausible. Karen tells me there's a St. Katy the Virgin who was a pig (again using the word in its original sense) but she can't remember any details. There is certainly a pig that goes to Heaven in *Der Heilige Antonius von Padua,* Wilhelm Busch's hilarious parody of the medieval Lives of the Saints. (He also originated the Katzenjammer Kids, way back in the last century; they were Max und Moritz then.) Science fiction fandom has an Order of St. Fantony. The most famous hallows in science fiction itself are surely Boucher's Aquin — though here again you're left in doubt whether the sanctity is real — and Miller's Leibowitz. Fritz Leiber's robots in *The Silver Eggheads* have a cult of saints with names like Karel and Isaac.

Not all are so pleasant. I once described an accursed church of St. Grimmin's-in-the-Wold, and a sonnet by H.P. Lovecraft warns you: "Beware St. Toad's cracked chimes." But of course the ultimately sinister figure in this subclass of dubiously benevolent imaginary saints is Trinian.

Some names lead me to wonder about their possible calendrical origin. Who was the St. Peter (Ste. Pierre) Smirnoff whose name adorns vodka bottles? Any killjoys who claim that "Ste." stands for "Société" and is a feminine form anyway, will please take their business elsewhere. I want to believe in some good, kind, white-bearded holy man who passed the miracle of turning water into vodka. Does St. Exupéry derive from a Christian named Exuperius, whom Nero martyred by shooting him from a catapult? St. Gaudens and St. Saëns likewise revive a flagging sense of wonder.

There are millions of St. Johns. About thirty years back, a Robert St. John was a well-known journalist and radio personality. He was also bearded, long before this was fashionable. The story goes that once he was waiting for a friend in a hotel lobby. A stranger came up and asked who he was. "I am St. John," he replied, a bit miffed at not being recognized. "Ah," said the stranger, "here for the Baptist convention, I suppose?" — I shall always think of him as St. John the Commentator.

Who is not to be confused with St. John the Persian, a writer of poems, or with that Burroughs illustrator, the late J. Allen, who is surely St. John of Barsoom.

The title of saint has sometimes been humorously bestowed, notably on Simon Templar. I'll close this piece with an anecdote which probably no one but Minnesotans and the omniscient Avram Davidson will appreciate. Years ago, the state university there had a physics professor named Anthony Zeleny, a very moral man who gave little lectures on the evils of smoking and drinking, in between differential equations. Now the tech students at Minnesota have an annual day of parades, ceremonies, and frolic, presided over by St. Patrick, the patron of engineers. (When he chased the snakes from Ireland, he invented the worm drive.) So one year a float came along bearing an enormous caricature statue of Professor Zeleny, cigarette in one hand, whisky bottle in the other, and gorgeous blonde on his knee. The float was labelled "St. Anthony Falls."

A PHILOSOPHICAL DIALOGUE

"Hey, a great idea for an essay!" exclaimed the lady. "A sure-fire attention-getter. Come out against God, motherhood, and apple pie, and in favor of sin and the man-eating shark."

"That's new?" answered the gentleman. "You must have a different angle —"

"I'll think of one. For instance, motherhood increases population pressure and the man-eating shark reduces it. Didn't you see George O.'s letter in *Analog*?"

"Yes. Really, though, darling, these days the position you want me to take is dismally conventional. Much more effective to declare in favor of God, motherhood, and apple pie, and against sin and the man-eating shark."

"Won't work. People would only say, 'That's him again, on his back-to-McKinley kick.'"

"You prefer Nixon? Having barely survived Johnson and Kennedy? But anyhow, brighteyes, I'm well aware that these days it is not necessary and certainly not sufficient to argue from fact and logic. Your grounds must be fashionable."

"Okay, let's hear."

"Snuggle closer, hm? Now let me think — Ah, yes.

"God. Well, after all, without God there wouldn't be churches, would there? And without churches, there wouldn't be any Social Gospel or Fathers Berrigan and Groppi or many other delightful features of our mod world. And besides, you know, God is real groovy. Like in *Playboy* a little while back, remember, they had this article proving what a swinger Jesus was. And man has to find Meaning — he has to get away from Dehumanizing Science — and, sure, you can find Meaning if you say Om often enough, but you can find it in First Corinthians too; and Christianity draws from so many different religions that it has more to offer than its predecessors, whose temple rites, shamans, and gods were generally pretty brutal; in other words, Christianity can drive you a lot crazier than ziggurats and witches and vile, vile Rimmon.

"Next — don't bother me, I'm trying to think — motherhood. You must realize that the concept involves more than simply farrowing. The image of Mother requires a child already in the world — a whole family, in fact, of which she is the serene, benign, tender but infinitely strong and patient center — to which she devotes her entire life, considering herself happy if at the end when she is old, her children kiss her work-worn hands before they set her little grandchildren on her lap that she may cuddle and care for these too. . . . Yes. Let's by all means associate reproduction with motherhood; let's get this fixed in every female heart and soul. The population curve will nosedive!

"Apple pie. . . . Don't bother me, I said. . . . Well, if you want to bother me *that* way —

"Ah, yes. Apple pie. Good old-fashioned American apple pie. None of these frozen imitations, produced by impersonal machines in some atmosphere-polluting factory for the profit of greedy capitalists. No, people should do for themselves, expressing their individuality in arts and crafts and apple pies. In fact, they ought to raise their own apples — and wheat, which they can personally plant, harvest, thresh, and mill — thereby helping the environment, since green leaves revitalize the air. . . . And having baked several extra pies, you can trade them to your neighbor for some wool off the sheep he keeps, which you can wash, card, spin, and weave with your own individual hands."

The gentleman stopped for breath. "What about the negative side?" asked the lady. "You're supposed to be against —"

"Sin. I know," he replied. "The kinds of sin being legion, let's stay by the nineteenth-century equation of it with fornication, and see if we can convince enlightened modern youth of the virtue of chastity. Hm-m-m. . . .

"One doesn't ordinarily get positive results by saying, when first introduced to a girl, 'How do you do? Do you fornicate?' At least, I never did, though I admit being too chicken to try. A certain amount of courtship is involved. And even after they have bedded, a couple must find things to do outside of this, or the relationship will perish of boredom and thus the fornication will stop.

"Therefore sinning takes time that could better be spent in demonstrating, rioting, and other socially conscious activities. It induces people to buy gifts for each other, making more profits for the corrupt establishment. They tend to drive around in automobiles, befouling the atmosphere. The mechanical contraceptives they throw away are not very bio-degradable. Or, if they use pills, these are produced in factories whose effluents doubtless go into the rivers.

"Obviously, the only way to be with it nowadays is to stay celibate."

"I am a hopeless reactionary," he reminded her.

"Really?" she murmured.

"You haven't finished," she said. "You've still got the man-eating shark."

"Forget it. A shark is not what I want right now — oh, all right. Simple. If man-eating sharks are around, people avoid swimming. This has several bad effects. For one, they don't get close to nature in that particular fashion. Instead, they stay in town, going to a movie or drinking in a bar or otherwise helping support the corrupt establishment. Furthermore, if they don't swim, they're less aware of the extent to which the water is polluted, and thus less likely to get active in the struggle to save our environment. And finally, when a shark does eat a man, it converts him to ordure, and too much untreated human waste is already being dumped into the oceans.

"Are you satisfied?"

"Not yet," she said.

"Same here," he agreed. "Let's stop talking and develop a meaningful relationship."

"Can't we just have fun?" she asked.

LOST SECRETS REVEALED

It is not always a sign of encroaching senility to growl that this or that is inferior to what it was in one's salad years. A fair-minded man admits that some progress, some improvement does get made. For instance, the miniskirt was a long step in the right direction. But then why should a fair-minded boy not admit that certain other things are not as good as they once were?

They just don't put the kind of stuff into hypotheses that they used to. Let me give you an example.

My personal memory lane is lined with Burma Shave signs. The fact that I must explain this to at least half the readership is a reminder of how many years have crept over me like wee red ants. An age seems to have passed since these things were. Their extinction was as sudden and startling, probably as sinister an omen, as the passing of the passenger pigeon.

Mind you, I have never actually approved of billboards. But a few did formerly possess a certain baroque charm. There were those which were put in an empty sagebrush desert by an auto repairman who styled himself Fearless Ferris, the Stinker, and used a skunk as his emblem. (No, my dear Society for Creative Anachronism, I don't remember whether it was couchant or rampant or piquant or what.) They had humor: e.g., outside of a hamlet named Battle Mountain, in the middle of optically flat hundreds of miles, one read APPROACHING BATTLE MOUNTAIN. USE SECOND GEAR.

And then there were the Burma Shave signs.

The product itself was a brushless shaving cream which came in squat jars. I never happened to use it — the advertising stopped before scraping my face had become a daily nuisance — and I was surprised to learn it was manufactured in Minneapolis where I lived. I imagine the stuff is no longer made, though perhaps it is; these days I generally employ a mowing machine. But the material is irrelevant, in the way that the flesh and blood of an artist are. He needs a body, of course, but his creations are the important thing. Likewise, as far as most people were concerned, the sole purpose of Burma Shave was to provide signs.

These always came in fives — small, discreet, though colored rectangles on low posts. They were exactly big enough and set at exactly the right intervals, one after the other, to be read with ease at what was then the average driving speed. The last always bore, simply, the legend BURMA SHAVE. The preceding four made a jingle. The meter varied little, and the rhyme scheme was an unchangeable abcb. However, the range of subjects was infinite.

Often a set merely advertised. Thus: "Shaving brush/In Army pack/Was straw that broke/This rookie's back./BURMA SHAVE." But frequently it promoted traffic safety, as in the macabre: "Approached a crossing/Without looking./Who will eat/His widow's cooking?/BURMA SHAVE." And sheer lightheartedness kept breaking through; thus: "Free, free,/A trip to Mars/For 10,000/Empty jars./BURMA SHAVE." (The story goes that somebody did collect that many, and the company was sportsmanlike enough to send him not to Mars, Pennsylvania but to Mars, Germany.) You, being a reader of mine and therefore alert and intelligent, will have noted that the fifth sign was a coda, never a part of the main composition. Surprisingly many persons at the time failed to grasp this, and produced such private bastardizations as "Never let your whiskers wave. Shave 'em off with BURMA SHAVE." The real form was rigidly structured as a villanelle or a limerick.

Except for the war years, no set remained long at any location; it would presently be replaced by a different quintet. And if you drove around the country a lot, you soon observed that the groups were not merely swapped — that is, no doubt they were to some degree, but old ones were gradually phased out and new ones appeared. In other words, the company surpassed Fred Hoyle; it had continual, if not continuous, creation *and* extinction, resulting in an equilibrium concentration of Burma Shave signs within a finite space.

Throughout our early boyhood, to my brother and me this was a fact of life, like the cycle of day and night. It's a sentimental myth that children wonder. They don't. They ask questions, but basically they absorb the world as it comes, without thinking. (Which reminds me of when Margaret Fuller stated grandly: "I accept the universe," and Thomas Carlyle, who happened to be on hand, was heard to snort, "Gad! She'd better!") The scientific temperament develops, if it ever does, only after puberty.

Sometime during our teens, John and I began actively inquiring into reality. We noticed the intrinsic strangeness of much we had hitherto taken for granted, like girls. Mysteries encompassed us. Who made the sun shine and the flowers grow, now that President Roosevelt was no more? Why is a planet when it spins? What is the meaning of "Perth Amboy"? Whither the pileated woodpecker? Whence came Burma Shave signs?

The alarming and significant fact grew in our awareness. We had never seen a quintet being changed. We did not know anyone who had. We could find no printed reference to anyone who claimed he had.

One morning you drove by the row, and it was different from what it had been, and that was all. No explanation. No predictable schedule. No traces of upheaval. Just: this.

Furthermore, a change was never reported in newspapers or on the steam radio. Officialdom never so much as discussed it, let alone attempted to exert any control — which is absolutely uncharacteristic of officialdom, especially with regard to so basic a part of the American scene. Right-wingers did not extol Burma Shave signs as a paradigm of success through free enterprise, nor did left-wingers denounce them as capitalistic exploitation of working men's eyeballs. Stephen Vincent Benét wrote no ballads about them. Ordinary folk like us would mention them in casual conversation, but the silence on higher levels was downright eerie. It became clear that a vast, all-pervasive, smooth-running Power was in control.

Being no more paranoid than is standard for adolescents, John and I did not assume the Power was evil. There must be excellent reasons for all the secrecy. Indeed, a quatrain would lose most of its force if its advent were heralded. Competitors might steal a march, did they know what was due in a certain area. Under the prevailing policy, they were always caught flat-footed and none of their own ads were really visible against the blinding psychological glare of BURMA SHAVE.

Thus, constructing our explanatory hypothesis, we chose what looked like the simplest assumptions. (Did William of Ockham use Burma?) To account for the facts, we needed to postulate little more than a huge and secretive organization.

Never mind where the cream factory was; as said, the actual stuff existed only for the sake of the verses. The sign production was something else. Doubtless this took place in an enormous, closely guarded cube of a building. With memories of the Manhattan Project and H.G. Wells' Morlocks, we could visualize how tight and harsh a security operation went on, and what untold tales of spies from Palmolive and thwarted raids by Mennenite gangs its steel-jacketed archives must hold. But this was secondary. As you could not have had an atomic bomb without physicists, so you could not have Burma Shave jingles without poets.

Surely these occupied the upper levels, and surely they dwelt in a hierarchy of Mandarin complexity and Byzantine intrigues. In a great, barnlike, coldly lighted chamber the has-beens and the never-would-bes sat desk by desk, pounding their typewriters to the monotonous beat of an overseer's gong. But that was mere mechanical testing of permutations, with some slight hope in addition of randomness producing an occasional useful phrase. Nowadays we would turn it over to a computer.

The true poets, the creators, had regular offices. Their supervisors rode close herd on them; conferences were frequent, with all the gray flannel sycophancy which it was then fashionable to believe pervaded the American business world. You didn't get to be the very least of these executive-rhymesters without a check of you, your family, and your relatives unto the thirteenth degree, thorough enough to turn J. Edgar Hoover first white, then green (never red) with envy.

And yet, as said, Burma Shave was by no means an evil organization. These measures were essential to its continued existence, and the bureaucracy and yessing were no worse than is inevitable under such circumstances. Ability was what really counted. You must be able to cut it; you must never let yourself get all lathered up; soft soap was no substitute for sharpness. Given traits like these, you could go far in Burma Shave.

Imagine how inspiration strikes a young poet. He sits alone, transfigured, for minutes or hours, before he plunges into feverish scribbling. He takes no paper away with him — what does not go into a safe overnight must be thrown down a chute to an electric furnace — but when he drives home, his words are seared into his brain. Having been cleared, he and his wife actually enjoy more privacy than most people; agents make regular checks to be sure that nobody has bugged their house. How impatiently he dithers through cocktails, and dinner, and a rattled newspaper, until at last the children are in bed and they dare talk about the matter!

Probably she give him some good ideas. Bright, up-and-coming men generally marry women who are also bright as well as beautiful. This couple knows that, should his basic concept be accepted, should it become a part of America, he is made. From then on he will have supervisor status, shares of stock will be given to him, and before he retires he may hope to sit upon the Board.

They steel themselves. They know what the odds are against the success of any single quatrain. And yet . . . and yet . . . Burma Shave allows, yea, it encourages all of its acolytes to dream. That night, husband and wife do not do so literally. They are far too excited to sleep.

For days thereafter, he is wrapped in his work — searching through thesauruses and rhyming dictionaries, trying hundreds of variations, striving to anticipate every conceivable objection and marshal every argument in favor. He grows abstracted, is no longer a jolly companion at lunch, begs off social engagements. His colleagues notice. They guess what the reason is, are jealous, seek excuses to drop in on him and sound him out. But he preserves silence, he whisks his papers into a drawer the instant the office door is opened, he holds back everything until at the end-of-the-week conference there comes his moment of truth.

I need not describe in detail the bombshell impact of his carefully diffident "notion I've been sort of kicking around, thought you fellows might maybe like to run up the flagpole," nor the sly attempts of Uriah Heep to discredit not only it but him, nor the bluff gallantry with which good old Mr. Bush rallies to his defense; and all the time the supervisor watches, listens, alert, enigmatic . . . but seeing that youth and hopefulness, do those cold eyes briefly soften as he remembers . . .?

In the end, the proposal goes Up Through Channels. Again I need not recount the haggling, the higgling, the useless changes made by every self-important nobody along the line who has somehow to justify his bloated salary. Nor need I write any Dostoyevskian account of the suspense, the anguish of the waiting, husband fretting himself into a shadow while wife gains back the thirty pounds she thought she had lost and children learn to speak, oh, very softly.

However slowly, however mutilated, the quatrain does at last reach The Top.

John and I supposed there had to be some ultimate authority. His office would of course be in a penthouse on the building. Despite the legion of secretaries and other underlings in the outer rooms of this suite, it would have a quietness intensified, in the inner sactum, by plush carpet, darkly glowing Rembrandts upon oak wainscoting, and that acre of polished rosewood and glass — broken only by an onyx pen-and-pencil set, an ivory telephone, a notepad at the precise middle, and a picture in a massive silver frame that no visitor ever actually saw — which was the desk of him whom the organization called (in hushed tones) The Big Burma.

He did not have many visitors, nor did that telephone ring very often; and when it did, the caller was more apt to be the president of Standard Oil or of the United States than any subordinate. The Big Burma expected those beneath him to handle any routine on their own. Woe betide them if they did not! His time was too precious to waste on details. (No one knew what he did spend it on.) Yes, he was a figure of mystery, a despot: but a benevolent one, who enjoyed scribbling his curt "OK" on certain of the poems which finally reached him.

And the rapture in the home of that hitherto humble scrivener! And the tortuous passage downward Through Channels! But at last — the Finalized Form, and tooling up in the factory division, and production under the watch of those grim, skilled guardsmen.

And meanwhile, the logistics teams buzz with plans. Heads grown gray in the service bend over reports and charts. Lean fingers trace routes out on great tabletop maps. A low, steady voice says, "It appears to me our optimum strategy is —" while faded blue eyes peer out of hawklike faces.

And the chosen night comes. Armored trucks grumble in their underground hangar, turning its air blue and acrid while mechanics give them their ultimate checkout. In the ready room the briefing of the drivers takes place, and of the relief drivers, and of those who will remove the old signs, and of those who will hammer in the new, and of those who, bleak-visaged, will ride shotgun. At length: "Very well, gentlemen. This is it. God bless you. Good shunting!" The cigarettes are tossed away, the chairs scrape back, feet boom on the floor, zippers rise scrittily on leather jackets. . . .

And the fleet roars out the gate and disperses. . .

Days afterward, the return, the debriefings, the evaluations, finally the records filed away because soon will come a new mission. . . .

I do not know if anything like the universe of The Big Burma ever existed. It just seemed like the most reasonable explanation of the facts. Not that it covered all of them. For instance, why *Burma* Shave? Once in youth, did he who sat in that lonely eyrie wander through the mysterious East and meet a wild, lovely Eurasian girl whom he never afterward could forget, even though she ran off to join Terry and the Pirates? Or what? The basic idea could be elaborated indefinitely. This potential is one characteristic of a good hypothesis, and I submit to you that nobody has made them that good since — for unknown but doubtless terrible reasons — BURMA SHAVE vanished, apparently forever, out of this world.

UNCLEAVISH TRUETHINKING

In the growth of world-knowledge, one of the most astounding forthfarings has been in the kingdom of stuff during the last hundredyear. We know that all stuff, even the thickest and hardest, is made up of many most-small things. It was thought at first that these were the smallest things of all, and could not be cloven further, so they were named unclefts. Up to 92 kinds of uncleft were known, from waterstuff, the least, to ymirstuff, the greatest. These kinds, which link together to form all others, were called *firststuffs*.

Today we know of more firststuffs, up to 104 at the last reckoning. Furthermore, we know that every firststuff is, in sooth, made up of more than one kind, each having its own weight though making the same links as the others. Thus, for an outshow, waterstuff has three known kinds, of weights 1, 2, and 3. These are called its *likesteads*, for that they hold the same steading on the round-around board of the firststuffs.

These unlike weights come from the little uncleft being made up of lesser bits. The heaviest deal of the uncleft is the *kernel*; it has nearly all the weight, and a forward lading. Around the kernel are the tiny bits called *flows*, which bear a backward lading. They are so named because they are what stirs in a wire or a salt wetblend whenever an amberish flowing goes through it. Once folk thought that the flows swing around the kernel like worlds around the sun; but as we shall see, now wisemen think otherwise.

The kernel itself is not a blank ball, but holds many bits. Of these, the lordliest are two: the forwardbits and the stillbits. Both weigh about 1800 times as much as the flow. The forwardbits have a forward lading, and in the kernel of the hale uncleft there are as many of them as there are flows outside. The stillbits have no lading. It is the tale of the forwardbits which says what kind of firststuff we have (one in the waterstuff kernel, 26 in the iron kernel, 92 in the ymirstuff kernel, and so on). The tale of stillbits says which likestead of the firststuff we have. Thus, there is no stillbit in the kernel of the lightest and oftest waterstuff likestead; but there is one stillbit in the kernel of the so-called "heavy waterstuff" or twainstuff, and two in the kernel of the seldom-found threestuff. This is why we say these have uncleavish weights of 1, 2, and 3.

Likewise, as we have said, iron always bears 26 forwardbits; but it may have anywhere from 27 to 33 stillbits, offhanging on which likestead we are handling with.

An uncleft may lose one or more flows, and so get a forward lading; or it may gain one or more, to win a backward lading. The unclefts of firststuffs link together to make what is called a *gang*. They do this by sharing flows in any of a clutch of unlike ways. For an outshow, the gang of water has two waterstuff unclefts bound to one sourstuff uncleft; the gang of rust has two iron and three sourstuff unclefts; but one of the many kinds of gangs which make up our own flesh may have thousands or even thousandthousands of unclefts in it (most of these being coalstuff, waterstuff, sourstuff, and chokestuff.)

From either the banding or the breaking asunder of gangs, we may get *work*, such as the heat and light of fire. Until lately, it was thought that only thus could work be gotten out of stuff itself; else we must get it from wind, tide, weight-pull, and so on.

Then about 60 years ago, wisemen learned that work is not gained or given off in a steady on-running, but in *chunks*. Even light comes in chunks, though it also behaves wavily. The work in a lightchunk is h (a small steadytale) times the oftenness of the light wave.

Soon after, it was found that room and time are blent into one, which we call room-time. This learning is known as the truethinking of kinship, for that it shows room, time, weight, work — indeed, all greatnesses — are akin and offhangy of each other. One outfollowing of this truethinking is that weight and work are naught but othersights of the same thing. Any stuff can be turned to work; and a lightchunk can be turned into a twain of uncleavish bits, one forward and one backward though of like weights. The law is: $W = ws^2$, or, in manspeech, work selflikens to weight times the speed of light foursided.

Somewhat later, world-knowledgemen showed that all the bits of stuff behave in some ways as if they were waves. The flow is not a hard ball wheeling around the kernel, but a shell of waves. These waves have heights answering to the likelihood of the bit being at that stead where the height is marked off. It had long been known that some likesteads break up of themselves, giving off hard light and/or bits, thus turning into other likesteads or firststuffs. This is called *light-rotting*. Now the wave truethinking shows that they do this for that there is a likelihood of a bit from the kernel being outside the uncleft altogether.

Today all men know that the kernel of the ymirstuff likestead of uncleavish weight 235 can be sundered by a stillbit, with much work unloosed as well as more stillbits to break up still more kernels of ymirstuff-235. This is called a *linked together-working*. It was the means whereby we first got use from that work which the truethinking of kinship had long said was locked in the uncleft. Since, we have come to know many other kinds of kernelish together-workings, among them the one in which four waterstuff unclefts are blent into one of sunstuff. This is thought to be what makes the stars shine. World-knowledgemen hope soon to tame it themselves, so that thrallwrights may put it at the bidding of mankind.

Soothly we live in a mighty time!

HERRINGS

Too often, what passes for realism is simply lack of imagination.

* * * *

Prolegomenon to a new theory of politics: Government is an essential self-protective device of society whereby its robbers, parasites, sadists, and busybodies are made to batten on it under some legal restraint.

* * * *

The pursuit of amusement has brought about more friendships, and better and more enduring ones, than work or war.

* * * *

The trouble with prostitution is that, like going to a movie on your first evening in a strange city, it is a confession of defeat.

* * * *

Art is the politics of the possible.

* * * *

In the country of the blind, the one-eyed man pays an optic tax.

* * * *

Live each day as if it were your first.

* * * *

Nothing is infinitely precious.

* * * *

The reason that many people oppose any further exploration of space is doubtless that what we find out there could make their pet causes look small.

* * * *

Asceticism is a luxury.

* * * *

Everybody is a conservative. The difference lies in what each of us wants to conserve.

* * * *

The optimum is not the perfect.

* * * *

In a world where untold millions of elaborately educated people still believe in astrology, we have no immediate hope of getting rid of Marxism.

* * * *

I can always break an awkward silence at a party by saying in a sententious voice, "Do you realize that 'Constantinople' spelled backwards is 'Elponitnatsnoc'?"

* * * *

To be loved is an awesome responsibility.

* * * *

I sometimes think we were created because the gods wanted to be entertained one evening by a farce — but no, that can't be. We are high comedy at least.